™

THE KING AND I ™

by Janet Quin-Harkin
From the Animated Motion Picture
adapted from the musical by
Richard Rodgers and Oscar Hammerstein II

SCHOLASTIC INC.

New York Toronto London Auckland Sydney
Mexico City New Delhi Hong Kong

ISBN 0-590-68065-X

© 1999 by Morgan Creek Productions, Inc.

All rights reserved. Published by Scholastic Inc.

SCHOLASTIC and associated logos are trademarks and/or registered trademarks of Scholastic Inc.

Interior design by Louise Bova

12 11 10 9 8 7 6 5 4 3 2 1   9/9 0 1 2 3 4/0

Printed in the U.S.A.

First Scholastic printing, March 1999

Contents

1 I Whistle a Happy Tune................1

2 The Palace of a
   Thousand Rooms.....................7

3 The King's "Very Scientific"
   Palace.................................12

4 The Servant Girl and
   the Kick Boxer......................17

5 Hello, Young Lovers
   Good-bye, Master Little...........20

6 A Letter from the Kralahome......25

7 There Are Nice Houses
   Outside the Palace!................29

8 Problems in the Palace............35

9 Anna Gives Advice.................41

10 A Very Civilized Banquet.........46

11 Flight into Danger...............54

12 The King to the Rescue!.........59

13 The Kralahome Strikes...........66

14 The Kralahome Hates
    Happy Endings....................70

Chapter 1

I Whistle a Happy Tune!

Long ago, before the age of giant ocean liners, a small sailing ship crossed the ocean. The sky was filled with dark storm clouds. Waves tossed the tiny ship up and down. Twelve-year-old Louis Leonowens held onto the rail while his eyes searched desperately: Where was Moonshee, the captain's pet monkey? Suddenly, he gave a cry of horror. Moonshee was clinging to the bowsprit at the front of the boat. He had climbed out there and was trapped by the big waves.

"Moonshee!" Louis yelled as the little monkey disappeared under the water. Louis didn't stop to think. He grabbed a rope and tied it around his waist. Then, inch by inch, he climbed out to grab the frightened monkey. Suddenly, a big wave swept them both away.

Louis's mother, Anna, was sitting in her cabin when she saw something fly past her porthole. "Louis!" she screamed.

She ran out of her cabin in time to see the sailors pulling the boy safely back on board. Louis was holding the wet, scared monkey.

Someone else had been watching Louis get pulled back to safety. In far-away Bangkok, in the land of Siam, a wicked magician called the Kralahome was watching the ship through his magic gong.

"Behold the King's new schoolteacher," he said to his short, rolypoly assistant, Master Little. He knew that Anna had been hired from Britain to teach the King's royal children, and the Kralahome wasn't happy.

"Do you know what she brings?" he asked.

"Homework?" Master Little tried to guess.

"Progress!" the Kralahome roared. "No more superstition. No more fear. No more *me*!"

"Are you going to scare her away, O Frightful One?" Master Little asked excitedly.

The Kralahome gave an evil smile. He had a more clever plan. "I'm going to make her hate Siam," he said. "I want her to think that the King of Siam is a barbarian. Then she'll tell the British and they'll come and take over Siam and find a new King."

"You?" Master Little asked, finally understanding what the Kralahome was thinking.

The Kralahome smiled again. "The storm has already created fears and doubts."

Master Little gulped.

"GIVE. ME. *GONG*," thundered the Kralahome.

Master Little struck the magic gong with all his might.

On the deck, Louis and his mother stood looking anxiously at the storm clouds. Suddenly, the clouds got darker and darker. The evil Kralahome had turned the clouds into a huge sea serpent! It covered the whole sky. Smoke and fire came out of its nose. Its eyes were glowing as it bent its head, closer and closer. . . . Anna stood bravely facing the cloud monster. She didn't seem to be scared.

"What do you do when you're frightened, Mother?" Louis asked in a trembling voice.

"I whistle," Anna said bravely. She stood up tall and began to sing,

Whenever I feel afraid
I hold my head erect
And whistle a happy tune,
So no one will suspect
                 I'm afraid.

Louis started to sing along with her. As they whistled, the serpent suddenly turned back into ordinary dark clouds. The Kralahome had *not* made them afraid.

"I think whistling is a very good idea, Mother," Louis said proudly.

"It *is* a very good idea, isn't it?" Anna agreed, putting her arm around her son.

"I don't think I shall ever be afraid again," Louis declared. But the evil magician was still watching in his magic gong. "Yes, you will," he hissed.

Chapter 2

The Palace of a Thousand Rooms

A few days later the ship sailed into Bangkok harbor. The captain let Louis look through his telescope. Louis gasped in horror — he thought he was looking at another sea serpent. But it was just a magnificent ship, carved like a dragon, coming to meet them.

Sitting under a golden canopy was an important-looking man.

"Is that the King?" Anna asked the captain.

"The prime minister, the Kralahome," the captain answered. He warned her to be careful. The Kralahome was very powerful.

The Kralahome seemed polite and friendly as he welcomed Anna and Louis, but little Moonshee was scared of him. Louis sadly handed the monkey back to his owner, the captain. They had become great friends during the long voyage.

"Maybe *you* should take the useless creature," the captain said, pretending that he didn't want the monkey anymore. Louis was overjoyed. His new life wouldn't be so strange if he had his monkey friend beside him.

Anna and Louis climbed onto the royal barge and sailed toward the city of glittering temples and palaces.

The King's palace was the most splendid of all. Louis looked up at the towering gold doors with marble elephants on either side of them. Inside were courtyards full of flowers and long marble halls. Suddenly, there was a loud clang. The doors had swung shut behind them. They were trapped in the palace whether they liked it or not!

Louis looked at his mother. She didn't seem afraid as they followed the Kralahome down a long hallway. "You'll be shown to your rooms," the Kralahome said to Anna.

"But," Anna said firmly, "the King promised me my own house, *outside* the palace."

"The King does not always remember his promises," the Kralahome replied.

"Then I must remind him," said Anna.

The Kralahome smiled to himself. This was going to be good — people who were rude to the King wound up gone!

At last they came to the most splendid room in the palace. A proud, dignified man sat on a golden throne. It was the King! At his side was his pet black panther, Rama. He stroked Rama as he received gifts from other lands. Anna was about to walk in and introduce herself but the Kralahome held her back.

"Wait. The King of Burma has sent a gift to His Majesty," he whispered.

Anna stared in horror when she realized that the "gift" was a beautiful young servant. "She's a *person,* not a rug," Anna hissed.

The Kralahome grinned at her. "A barbaric old custom," he whispered. "The King loves it."

As the trembling servant was led away, Moonshee made a dive for the Burmese ambassador's turban. He thought the fruit on it was real. Instead it was made of precious stones. The ambassador yelled as Moonshee danced away with a handful of jewels. Palace guards leaped forward. Their swords were drawn. Louis didn't think about the danger. He had to save Moonshee from certain death! He flung himself between the swords, but too late. Moonshee dashed on until he came face-to-face with . . . Rama the panther. Rama growled. Scared, Moonshee leaped among the piles of presents that collapsed and fell.

At last Louis managed to grab the monkey. He looked up to see a guard with a sword raised — about to cut off his head!

Chapter 3

The King's "Very Scientific" Palace

At the last moment the King held up his hand as Anna raced to stand in front of her son.

"Who? Who? Who?" the King demanded.

"Your Majesty, he meant no harm," Anna pleaded.

The King bent down to Louis. "Never hide behind a woman's skirt," he whispered. "It is not brave. Also, it's impossible to know when she will sit down."

Then he stood up again and pointed to Anna.

"I am Anna Leonowens, your majesty. The schoolteacher you sent for from England," Anna said. "There is a matter we must settle. . . ." She tried to tell him about the house she had been promised but the King ignored her.

"Good," he declared. "You are part of my plan to bring Western culture to Siam. Come."

He grabbed her arm and pulled her along, down hallways and into . . . a science lab. Anna couldn't have been more surprised. Inside the lab Siamese scientists in white coats were working with the King's latest inventions. The King proudly showed her his printing press, which was wheezing and clanking dangerously. "First modern Siamese book," he said proudly. "*A Short History of the Royal Family.* Author: myself."

Next he pointed to a bamboo version of a steam engine, then giant rockets, and last, his pride and joy — a model hot air balloon. "Air travel is future," he said grandly.

Moonshee chose that moment to escape from Louis again. He found a silk rope on the floor and tugged at it. The balloon sailed up into the air, carrying Moonshee with it, crying in fright. As the air came out of the balloon, it swooped and dove around the room. Louis grabbed Moonshee as everyone else ran for cover back to the throne room.

"Still working on details," the King said as he slammed the door shut. He began to walk around Anna, looking at her.

"You do not look like teacher person," he decided. "How old shall you be?"

"A hundred and fifty years, Your Majesty," Anna replied calmly.

The King's eyes sparkled. He could play that game too. "In what year were you born?" he snapped.

"In 1712," Anna replied quickly.

The King was enjoying this game. He asked her about her children and grandchildren, but she had an answer for everything. At last she managed to remind him about his promise to build her a house.

"You teach in palace. You live in palace," the King roared. He stormed out of the room.

"I tried to warn you," the Kralahome whispered to Anna.

Suddenly, she cried out. Her trunks were being carried away. "Stop. Those are mine," she called and ran after them. But the Kralahome stepped out to stop Louis from following her. "This is a good moment to

show a young man the royal armory
where the weapons are kept," he said
to Louis.

Then he whispered to his servant
Master Little, "And if he gets hurt,
the King will be blamed."

Master Little got the message. He
had to make sure an accident hap-
pened to Louis!

Chapter 4

The Servant Girl and the Kick Boxer

In the palace gardens a young girl sat crying. It was Tuptim, the servant girl newly arrived from Burma. She was lonely and frightened in the strange palace. Suddenly, something tapped her on the shoulder, making her jump. She turned to see a little elephant with a broken tusk.

"I bet some hunter did that to you," she said angrily. "I shall call you Tusker." She didn't know that Tusker was the son of the King's royal white elephant.

She picked a banana for Tusker. Now at least she had one friend here.

A shout behind the hedge made her look up. She peered through the leaves. Two strong young men were practicing kick boxing, a sport that was very popular in Siam. Without warning one of the young kick boxers looked in Tuptim's direction. Their eyes met. Tuptim gasped and ran away. The young man followed as Tuptim tried to hide behind one bush, then another.

Tusker wasn't interested in playing hide-and-seek. He was hungry. He sniffed at the banana peel, then threw it away just as the young man came running. Whoops! The young man skidded on the peel and landed on his back. Tuptim tried not to laugh.

"Are you hurt?" she asked.

He got to his feet. "Just my pride," he admitted. "Who are you?"

Tuptim told him that she had been given as a present to the King. If she displeased him in any way she'd be sent home again — and that meant disgrace, dishonor, and possibly even death. The young man nodded sadly. He understood how hard it must be for her.

"What do you do here?" Tuptim wanted to know.

The young man hesitated. Then he said, "I serve the King, too." They laughed together, sharing their new friendship.

Chapter 5

Hello, Young Lovers Good-bye, Master Little

Anna had finally caught up with her boxes and trunks, in the women's quarters. Some of the ladies of the royal court came to look at her Western clothes.

"Welcome to your rooms, Mrs. Anna," Lady Thiang said.

"Please don't unpack my things,"

Anna instructed. "I'm not staying." But the women were very curious. They wondered if Anna really had legs under her wide skirts. Anna lifted her skirt to show them.

Another of the women had found a photo. Anna snatched it back quickly. It was a photo of her dead husband. The women were surprised that even a schoolteacher could have known true love. Anna went over to the window and looked out. Down in the garden she saw Tuptim and the kick boxer together. They seemed so happy to have found each other. It reminded her what it was like to be young and in love. Lady Thiang came over to the window to look, too. She let out a horrified gasp. "S-s-s-servant girl and Crown Prince!" she stammered. "Is forbidden. Against tradition!"

While Anna was watching the young lovers in the garden, Louis had arrived at the armory with Master Little. It was a room full of dangerous weapons. Louis was excited.

"Do they still work?" he asked.

That was exactly what Master Little meant to show him. . . .

But Moonshee was smart. He knew just what was in Master Little's head.

As Master Little toppled a stack of sharp axes onto Louis, Moonshee pushed him out of the way.

Louis didn't even see the axes fall inches behind him. He was too interested in the crossbows. He touched the trigger and *wham* — an arrow shot across the room right over Master Little's head.

"Good thing Master Little is so little," the Kralahome's hapless servant said.

"Sorry," Louis said and went over to look at the suits of armor.

Master Little tried to grab a spear to throw at Louis, but instead the whole pile of spears came down on top of *him*.

Master Little was getting angry now. He charged at Louis with a raised club — just as Louis decided to practice spear throwing. He drew back his arm . . . and the butt of his spear hit Master Little on the nose, making him drop the club on his own head. Ow!!

It wasn't Master Little's day. No matter what he tried, he couldn't make an accident happen to Louis. In frustration he grabbed the deadly spiked balls on chains. He twirled them around his head, ready to throw them at Louis. But Moonshee was still watching out for his young master. He tickled Master Little under his arm. Master Little collapsed in giggles and the balls wrapped themselves around his neck. Louis was very interested.

"Wow. Can you do that again?" he asked.

Chapter 6

A Letter from the Kralahome

Trumpets sounded to call everyone to the throne room. The King sat on his throne and clapped his hands. One by one the royal children came to be presented to Anna. There were the Princesses, Kannika, Naomi, Manya, and the adorable Ying; as well as Prince Ratsami and the identical twins, Prince Thoni and Prince Moni. They came one by one to their father and bowed low. Then they knelt on the floor. Last of all came Prince Chululongkorn, the King's heir, walking proudly with his head held high. Anna gasped. She recognized the young kick boxer from the garden.

Although Anna was determined not to stay, when she looked at all the hopeful young faces, she knew she couldn't leave them. She took off her bonnet. The King gave a satisfied nod. "The schoolteacher will stay," he announced. "Will live in palace."

"For the time being, Your Majesty," Anna agreed. She didn't want the King to think he had won.

The royal children were happy. So was the Kralahome. Now he could go on with his plan to get rid of the King.

That night he met with Master Little secretly in the royal elephant

The King of Siam was a strong ruler, and a good, but proud man. He asked Anna, a British schoolteacher, to teach the royal children about the modern world. But sometimes, independent Anna and the traditional King don't see eye-to-eye.

The royal children [left to right]
Prince Thoni, Princess Naomi,
Prince Monti, Prince Ratsami,
Princesses Kannika and Manya,
were surprised to find out that
Siam is not the biggest country
in the world!

From her balcony in the palace, Anna looked into the garden. Watching a pair of young lovers, she remembered her own great love. But Lady Thiang is upset—for *this* young love is forbidden.

The couple in the garden was the King's son, Crown Prince Chululongkorn, and Tuptim, the young servant girl. They were falling in love.

The Crown Prince gave Tuptim the royal pendant as a token of his love. He defied the old traditions—especially the one where the King chooses a bride for his son.

When the King ordered Tuptim punished, she ran away with the Crown Prince. Louis and his pet monkey Moonshee followed. But with Anna's guidance, the King realized he was wrong, and risked his life to save all of them from the Kralahome's evil sorcery.

Prince Chululongkorn and Tuptim rode the King's royal white elephant to safety, while Louis and Moonshee followed on Tusker's back. When they stopped short, Tusker accidentally plowed right into the royal elephant's backside.

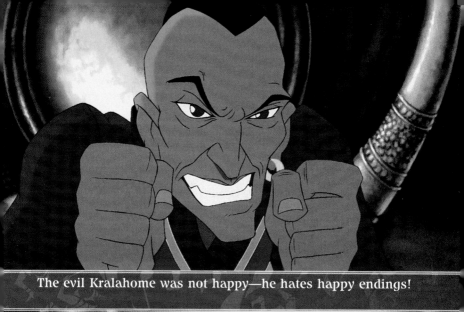

The evil Kralahome was not happy—he hates happy endings!

And anything that doesn't please the Kralahome doesn't please his assistant, Master Little!

"Shall we dance?" Anna asked her new friend, the King. They did—and lived happily ever after.

stables. He instructed Master Little to write a letter to the British. "To Sir Edward Ramsay, British envoy," he dictated. "Your schoolteacher is in grave danger. . . ."

When the letter was complete, the Kralahome turned to the elephants with a greedy smile. "When I become King, I'll sell your tusks for ivory," he snarled at them. He pointed to the great white elephant, Tusker's father. "I'll start with you." He laughed. The royal white elephant trumpeted in anger.

The Kralahome fastened the letter closed with a golden seal and sent Master Little to mail it.

Far away in Singapore Sir Edward Ramsay stood on the deck of a British gunboat. He was looking forward to going home to England. He was about to take afternoon tea with the captain when he noticed the letter, lying on a silver tray. He managed to grab it before it was blown into the ocean. When he read it he gasped in horror. "My dear Anna is in danger," he exclaimed. "Change course, Captain. We're going to Siam to depose a barbaric King!"

Chapter 7

There Are Nice Houses Outside the Palace!

When Anna was getting ready for school the next day, Tuptim came into her room, carrying fresh flowers. Anna felt sorry for the young servant girl. She gave her a book of poetry. Tuptim was frightened — servants were forbidden to read. Anna could get into trouble for giving her the book. Anna wasn't scared. "I'm a teacher, not a servant," she said. "I can do as I please."

Then she heard a gong. She mustn't be late for school on her first day. She hurried to the schoolroom. The children were waiting for her, all sitting on the floor, except for the Crown Prince. He had his own desk, decorated with jewels.

The first thing Anna showed her pupils was a modern map of the world. It was unlike anything the royal children had ever seen. They were confused and angry.

"Siam is not so small!" the Crown Prince said.

"England is even smaller," Anna pointed out to him.

"But it's the center of the empire," Louis added proudly.

"Royal Siamese palace is center of whole universe," the Crown Prince countered.

"Everyone thinks their own home

is the center of the universe," Anna said wisely.

The children were interested to learn that not everyone lived in a palace. They had never been outside the walls before. Anna decided to show them how ordinary people lived. She led them to the palace gate. The children were afraid to go outside, until Louis went first. The Crown Prince wasn't going to be outdone by Louis. He went through the gate, too. Then all the children followed.

High in a palace room the Kralahome was watching Anna and the children. He told Master Little to go and follow them.

The children were having a wonderful time, learning all about the real world outside the palace and getting to know Anna. They saw market stalls and temples. They went into a silk factory to watch silk being spun and dyed. They made friends everywhere they went. Master Little hurried to catch up with them — but he fell into a vat of colored dye! The children walked on, unaware that he was following them.

Anna led them out of town, through the rice paddies where water buffalo were plowing. Master Little hid in the nearby jungle to watch them, until he was chased away by large snakes. He caught up with them just as they came back to the palace.

Meanwhile the Kralahome went to find the King. The King was working on his hot air balloon in the science lab.

"Your Majesty is so interested in science and education," the Kralahome said with a bow.

"How is the new teacher doing?" the King asked him.

The Kralahome crept closer. "She follows your example of breaking with old traditions," he said. "She has just taken the royal children outside of palace. . . ."

"The royal children outside of palace?" The King ran out angrily just in time to see Anna coming back with the royal children, now dirty and dusty with dye-stained fingers.

He was very angry.

"I thought the children should learn how people live outside the palace," Anna explained.

"Tell me something important you learn," the King said, pointing to Princess Kannika.

The little girl was afraid, but said, "There are nice houses outside the palace, Father."

Then the King realized what Anna was doing. She was not going to let him forget that he had promised her a house outside the palace. He reminded her that she was only his servant.

"Oh, no, Your Majesty, I am *not* your servant," Anna said in a shocked voice. "If you do not give me the house you promised me, I shall return to England."

The children gasped in horror at her boldness, but Anna didn't stop. "I can't stay in a country where promises have no meaning," she went on. "You talk about change but everything has to go according to your wishes."

The King stormed out angrily. The Kralahome appeared at Anna's side. "I tried to tell you," he whispered. "He is so barbaric. But don't worry. I'll help you. . . ."

"Don't bother," Anna snapped. "I'm leaving."

Chapter 8

Problems in the Palace

Back in her room, Anna started packing again. She threw her belongings into the suitcases while she said exactly what she thought of the King. The problem with him was that he was spoiled! He might have good ideas, but it wasn't good for him to have all those people bowing to him like toads. She kicked her trunk shut with satisfaction.

In the throne room the King was still angry with Anna. His son, the Crown Prince, challenged him. How could he be a modern King if he wouldn't change from the old ways?

The King had to think about this. What did his son mean?

"For example," the young Prince said carefully. "If you were a modern, scientific King, would you still choose a wife for your son?"

"Of course," the King snapped. "How can a boy be wise enough to choose a good wife?"

"It's possible," the boy suggested.

"One day you will be King," the King told his son. "Then you will know everything."

"But if I love someone . . ." the Prince began, then wisely kept quiet.

"Love has nothing to do with tradition," his father told him. He took his royal ivory pendant and put it over the Prince's head. That meant he would be King someday.

When the Prince left, the King was thoughtful. He went into the temple to think and pray. His pet panther, Rama, accompanied him. The temple was a wonderful building, lined with the statues of legendary warriors and revered leaders. At the far end was a beautiful emerald Buddha.

The King walked along the line of statues, thinking out loud. When *his* father was King, everything was easy. But now the whole world was changing. He was not sure who to trust. Should he join other nations or keep Siam alone?

He didn't know that the Kralahome was watching him through his magic gong. As the wicked prime minister struck the gong, the statues in the temple magically came to life. They crept up behind the King, ready to kill him. Rama, the panther, saw the danger his master was in. As the King prayed, Rama pushed him out of harm's way and drove the statues back to the walls again.

The King came to a decision. He had to go on being the leader of his kingdom, doing the best that he could do.

He stood up. "Prayer is so peaceful," he said to Rama. Rama sighed. So did the Kralahome, frustrated yet again.

In the gardens Louis was chasing Moonshee again. "Moonshee, the ship will sail. I don't want to leave you behind," he yelled.

As Louis ran through the bushes he saw the Prince, practicing his kick boxing again. The match ended.

"You are the champion again," the Prince's opponent said.

"Only because everyone is scared to hit you," Louis told the Prince.

The Prince was horrified.

"Come on. Let me try," challenged Louis. He started dancing around. The Prince didn't take Louis seriously. Suddenly, *bop!* Louis hit him on the nose. It started to bleed. Louis realized what he had done.

"It was just a lucky punch," he said, scooping up Moonshee.

The Prince felt bad. He realized Louis had been right. All this time his opponents had let him win. He went to wash his face in a pool. There he saw Tuptim.

"Are you hurt?" she asked. Then she gasped. The Prince was wearing the royal pendant. All at once, she knew who he was.

"I was afraid to tell you," he whispered.

Tuptim tried to run away. "Is forbidden," she said.

The Prince wouldn't let her go. He knew that he loved Tuptim. He held her in his arms and put his royal pendant around her neck. He promised to tell his father about them.

As he left the garden, Lady Thiang was looking for him. "The King has had bad news," she said. The Prince rushed to his father's side.

Master Little had been hiding in the bushes, watching the whole thing. He couldn't wait to tell the Kralahome. But Tusker had been there, too. He chased Master Little with his one sharp tusk. Master Little had to climb up into a mango tree and Tusker kept him trapped up there.

Chapter 9

Anna Gives Advice

Anna was finishing her packing when the Prince knocked on her door. "Mrs. Anna, I am worried," he said. "The British are coming to take over Siam. They say Father is a barbarian."

"That's outrageous," Anna said angrily. "Your father is not a barbarian!"

"Then will you go to him?"

"I can't go without being asked. You know that," Anna said sadly. The Prince left in despair. After he had gone Anna tried to decide what to do. The King made her angry, but he was trying hard to do the best for his country.

That evening Anna went into the throne room. The King looked up. "Good. You have come to apologize. I accept."

Anna tried to stop herself from losing her temper again.

The King was lying on a couch. "Have you no respect?" he asked. "Your head shall not be higher than King's."

"I can't grovel," Anna said proudly.

"You are difficult woman," the King sighed. But he sat up and Anna sat beside him.

"Do you have anything you'd like to talk about?" she asked, knowing that the proud King would not ask for advice. "Has there been any . . . news . . . recently?"

"News!" the King exploded. "They call me barbarian!"

"It's a lie," Anna said angrily. "What have you decided to do about it?"

"Guess," the King said.

Anna guessed he was asking her advice. "I believe you'll invite the British to the palace to show them the truth."

"I will?" the King asked.

"You'll entertain them with a banquet. Show them how civilized you are."

The King looked excited. "I'll show them most scientific experiment — air travel."

"And a ball? With dancing?" Anna suggested.

"You will arrange it." The King pointed at Anna. "One week."

All this time the Kralahome had been listening outside the door. He wasn't pleased with what he heard. He had to do something. He went to find Master Little. Master Little still sat trapped in the mango tree. At last it seemed that the elephant had gone away. He crept down and tried to get away when mangoes came flying at him. Moonshee and Tusker peppered him with flying fruit all the way back to the palace.

"Where have you been?" the Kralahome asked angrily.

Master Little was too exhausted to talk. He pantomimed that he had been watching kick boxing. Then he saw the Prince kissing the servant girl and giving her the royal pendant.

"Perfect," the Kralahome said, rubbing his hands together in delight.

"The British watching our King's every move, and, surprise, a servant girl has the royal pendant! What can His Majesty do but sentence her to a barbaric death?"

Chapter 10

A Very Civilized Banquet

Anna worked hard to prepare for the visit by Sir Edward, the British envoy. She tried to teach the royal cooks how to prepare British food without their Siamese hot sauce. She picked roses from the garden to make the guests feel at home. She even had Western-style gowns made for all the ladies of the royal court, and taught each woman how to walk and sit in a hoop skirt without tripping.

The King was also preparing. He was trying to learn how to eat with a knife and fork. His new hot air balloon was being readied for a demonstration and there was going to be a fireworks display, too.

At last everything was ready. The big British gunboat sailed into the harbor. Anna joined the King on the balcony to wait for the guests.

"Here." The King gave Anna a slip of paper. "List of subjects on which I am very brilliant and will make great impression."

Anna took off her cloak and the King's eyes opened wide. She was wearing a ball gown. Her shoulders were bare.

"Is that . . . customary?" he asked.

"I'm sorry Your Majesty doesn't approve," Anna said.

"I didn't say I do not approve," the King answered. "In England do women dance in the arms of men not their husband — dressed like that? I would not permit."

Anna's eyes lit up. She remembered when she went to balls and danced. She told the King what it was like to dance.

She sang and danced into the ballroom alone, followed by the King. Suddenly she stopped, feeling self-conscious.

"Why do you stop?" the King asked.

She told the King that a woman would never dance alone.

"But she will dance in arms of strange man?" the King asked.

"Not always a strange man," Anna said. "Sometimes a very good friend."

She and the King stared at each other. He was about to ask her to dance when the ballroom doors burst open. Sir Edward Ramsay stormed in, talking worriedly to the Krala-home, who was dressed for the occasion in an English tuxedo.

"Anna, are you all right?" he asked, striding across the room to her side. "I've been told this King is a barbarian," he muttered to her.

"Who? Who? Who?" The king didn't like this private talk.

Anna introduced Sir Edward. He'd been an old friend before she was married. The King was suddenly jealous. He clapped his hands.

"Dinner. Then dancing," he announced.

"A banquet in your honor, Edward," Anna added.

Sir Edward was amazed. He offered Anna his arm to go in to dinner. The King quickly copied the gesture. Anna hesitated but took the King's arm and went into the banquet.

The banquet hall had been transformed into an English dining room. The long tables were laid out as they

would have been in England —
white tablecloths, candles, and pol-
ished silverware. Sir Edward was
impressed as he sat beside the King
and Anna.

The meal started. Soup was placed
in front of the guests. The King picked
up his bowl but caught Anna's look.
Quickly she picked up her spoon. The
King picked up *his* spoon. The guests
followed. All through the meal the
King watched Anna to see what he
should do next. After the King got
used to his knife and fork, the meal
started to go well.

Anna got the King to talk about
all the things he had invented, the
book he had written, and his prized
hot air balloon.

Sir Edward now believed that he
had made a mistake. The King
wasn't a barbarian — he was a very
modern man.

The Kralahome realized he had to

work fast. When the talk turned to elephants, the Kralahome mentioned the sacred white elephant. He said that only the King can own such an elephant and he wears the royal ivory pendant made from a white elephant's tusk.

Sir Edward was curious to see the pendant, but the King had given it to his son. "Show!" the King commanded.

The Prince turned pale. How could he show the pendant when he had given it to Tuptim?

"Show!" the King roared again.

"I gave it away," the Prince stammered.

"Who? Who? Who?" the King demanded.

The Kralahome signaled to the guards. Tuptim was brought in, struggling. The King was furious. He snatched the pendant from Tuptim's neck, breaking the chain. "Dishonor!" he yelled. "Servant girl and Prince! Do as custom demands! Whipped . . . till death."

Anna and Sir Edward were horrified. Anna pleaded with the King but he was so angry that he wouldn't listen to her. He grabbed the whip himself. Anna stood close by. "I thought you were a good man, but now I know you are a barbarian," she cried. "I'll watch every single blow!"

The King raised the whip, then he lowered it again. He couldn't do it with Anna watching him.

"Send her back to Burma!" he commanded, looking at Tuptim.

"No, she'll be killed," the Prince begged. He leaped out and kick boxed down the nearest guard. Then he grabbed Tuptim's hand and they ran. Louis scooped up Moonshee, ready to follow them. His mother shouted after him, but he ran after his friends.

"Bring them back!" the King roared.

The Kralahome bowed. He gave orders to Master Little and the guards. "Make *sure* there is an accident this time," he commanded. "Then bring back their bodies!"

Chapter 11

Flight into Danger

The Prince, Tuptim, and Louis,
still clutching Moonshee, ran
over the palace rooftops. At last they
could run no farther. They had come
to the palace wall. Below them was a
terrible drop. They were trapped.
When they looked back they saw

fierce guards running after them, coming closer and closer. Louis staggered and lost his balance. The Prince grabbed him but lost his own balance. Tuptim grabbed at him, but it was no use. They plunged down from the terrible height.

Suddenly, they were lifted up into the air — on elephant trunks. Tusker and his father, the great white elephant, had saved them. They fled from the palace on the elephants' backs, out into the jungle.

Louis was very scared. He tried to whistle but his mouth was too dry.

Inside the palace the Kralahome was watching them through his magic gong. He struck the gong. The runaways suddenly found the path ahead of them blocked with a giant spiderweb. In the web was a horrible spider with glistening eyes. The elephants turned around and ran back again. None of them saw the spider shrink back to normal size as soon as they had gone. It was only one of the Kralahome's tricks.

They rushed along another path and ran right into Master Little, waiting for them with the guards.

"Reverse, where's reverse?" Louis yelled.

They tried another path, only to meet terrible roaring tigers. As they backed away, the tigers changed back into ordinary jungle mice — another Kralahome trick!

At last the Prince, Tuptim, and Louis came to a dangerous rope bridge, crossing high above a raging river.

"I hope it's safe," Tuptim said.

"*I'll* give you safe!" the Kralahome muttered as he struck his gong again. Instantly the holes in the bridge were filled in with imaginary planks of wood.

"I'll make sure," the Prince said

bravely, but the big elephant pushed past the Prince. He was the heaviest. He was going to try first. He made it across safely and beckoned with his trunk for the others to follow. Tusker went across next, then the Prince, holding Tuptim's hand. They had just crossed when flaming arrows fell around them. Master Little and the guards had caught them again. The support ropes of the bridge started to burn. Louis and Moonshee were still waiting to cross. As Louis ran across, the planks disappeared. He fell through and reached out for a dangling piece of wood. Moonshee ran up Louis's back, onto the bridge, and grabbed Louis's hand as it slipped.

"Don't wait for me," Louis yelled to the others, but the Prince ran back to help him. Tuptim tried to help too. They tried to pull Louis back onto the burning bridge as the evil guards closed in on them. The bridge collapsed and everyone plunged into the rapids below.

As Louis, Moonshee, and the Prince hit the water, they managed to hang onto pieces of wood from the bridge. They climbed onto a big piece of the bridge and used it for a raft. Tuptim climbed onto another piece — and they were swept down the rapids, faster and faster.

Chapter 12

The King to the Rescue!

The King went alone into the temple to pray. He was ashamed of what he had done and worried about his son.

"Can a King be wrong?" he asked the statue of Buddha. "What shall I do?" Then he made a big decision. "If

I find the children, I will show Mrs. Anna that I am sorry. . . ."

But how could he find the children, out there somewhere in the jungle? An idea began to dawn. He was a man of science. He had a way to search for the children!

Sir Edward Ramsay paced angrily at the window. "When I make my report, a whole fleet of boats will come here," he said to Anna. "That is the end of this King. He's not . . . a gentleman!"

He stopped talking. He and Anna ran to the window. A wonderful hot air balloon was going past. The King and Rama were in it. He was going to try to rescue his son!

The Prince, Moonshee, Louis, and Tuptim clung desperately to their rafts as they were swept down the rapids. But the guards were also on rafts, catching up with them. The

Prince knocked out an attacker who was about to harm Louis. Louis turned and kick boxed more guards. *Bam! Bam! Bam!*

"You learn fast," the Prince said, impressed.

Then Tuptim spotted a larger raft big enough for them all. They jumped on board, only to find it was another of the Kralahome's tricks. It melted away and they landed in the water.

"You are learning my true powers," the Kralahome chuckled as he watched them in his magic gong. They were about to swim to the bank and safety but the Kralahome changed the logs on the bank to crocodiles. Quickly they swam toward the opposite bank.

As they swam into calmer water they saw that there was a very old temple on the shore. It was the ruins of the Ancient Place of Elephants. There were statues of elephants everywhere, including a huge fountain with spouting elephants. Suddenly, the elephants came to life, smashing out with their trunks. The swimmers screamed as they were carried into the mighty mouth of a huge stone elephant.

It was like being in a water roller coaster. Louis held his breath until the giant statue spat him out. The Prince came shooting out after him, but Master Little was waiting for them with his crossbow raised.

Louis started to whistle. "Is not time to whistle," the Prince said, but Louis kept on whistling. Suddenly, two blasts of water knocked Master Little over. It was Tusker and his father.

"I was whistling to call them," Louis explained.

At that moment Tuptim came shooting out into the river, but she was swept away before they could grab her. "Get her!" the Prince yelled.

On the elephants' backs they raced down the riverbank, trying to grab Tuptim. But at last they could go no farther. A giant cliff loomed up ahead of them. The river plunged into a deep ravine. If Tuptim was carried down there, there was no hope for her. The Prince slid down the white elephant's trunk and leaned out as far as he could.

High above in the balloon, the King had spotted his son.

"Son, no!" he yelled.

Tuptim was swept past the Prince. Their fingertips almost touched as the Prince leaped in after her. The King signaled to Rama to pull the string to open the vent. Hot air rushed out. The balloon sank lower and lower. It was rushing toward the cliff face. At the last second the King leaned out and grabbed his son. The balloon started to rise again.

"Father. Save Tuptim," the Prince pleaded.

Tuptim held out her hand before she would be carried to her doom. The King hesitated, then reached down to save her.

Desperately Rama turned up the hot air burner with his tail and puffed hot air into the balloon. It started to rise, but could it rise quickly enough to make it over the cliff? Louis watched from Tusker's back as the balloon cleared the clifftop by inches. They were safe!

The Kralahome had watched the whole thing in his magic gong.

"I hate happy endings!" he screamed in anger. He hit the gong with all his might. Then he stared in horror. A crack appeared in the gong. It spread. More cracks appeared. The gong fell to pieces at the Kralahome's feet.

But the Kralahome refused to be beaten. "It's not over yet," he muttered as he ran out of his room.

Anna and Sir Edward were standing on the balcony. She was so happy to see Louis appear on Tusker's back. But suddenly she noticed a figure slinking up a flight of steps. It was the Kralahome. Anna decided to follow him. Then she gasped. She realized what the Kralahome was planning. The King's balloon appeared in the sky and the Kralahome was heading for the fireworks display with its big rockets!

Chapter 13

The Kralahome Strikes

Anna ran up the steps as fast as she could, trying to catch the Kralahome. The Kralahome was too fast for her. He reached the top of the steps and slammed the heavy iron gate in her face.

"You're too late," he laughed as he turned the key.

Anna watched helplessly as the Kralahome crouched beside a giant rocket. As the King's balloon came closer, he lit the fuse. The rocket roared up into the sky. The King saw the rocket coming and bravely flung himself in front of the others as the rocket exploded.

The balloon was damaged and began to sink.

"Jump," the King commanded while they were still over the water.

Tuptim and the Prince jumped into the safety of the water.

"You too," the King commanded his faithful panther. Rama didn't want to jump and leave his beloved master. So, to save Rama, the King had to lift him and drop him into the water!

The King was about to jump to safety when the Kralahome lit the fuse for the rest of the fireworks display. A rocket smashed into the balloon. The balloon fell from the sky like a stone.

"Good-bye, Your Majesty," the Kralahome snarled with a satisfied smile.

Anna rushed down the stairs. A crowd had gathered around the crushed balloon. As the torn fabric was pulled away, the King's body lay on the ground, deathly still. Rama gave his master's face a lick. The King didn't stir. Then the crowd parted for Anna. She knelt beside the King's body and reached out a hand to stroke his forehead. Tears welled up in her eyes.

Suddenly, the King's eyes snapped open. "I will say when is time to cry!"

Anna laughed through her tears.

The King was carried to his bedroom. He was still very weak and nobody knew if he would live or die. Anna sat beside him as he called in the Crown Prince.

"If I don't get better, you'll be the King," he said. "What would you do if you were King?"

The Crown Prince hesitated. Then

he said, "I would let everybody have books. Education is a good thing. And nobody should have to bow like toads. And all persons should marry who they want . . . even royal Prince."

He looked across to the door. Tuptim came in, dressed like a beautiful Princess. The Prince held out his hand to her. Anna held her breath.

Then the King said, "Why should royal Prince have less rights than anyone else?"

He smiled at his son. "You will be a great King," he said.

Chapter 14

The Kralahome Hates Happy Endings

Not everyone was happy that the King was recovering and the Prince had found his true love. The Kralahome and Master Little were now working in the elephant stables. The great white elephant and Tusker grinned and trumpeted as they watched the men cleaning out the smelly stables. Louis smiled too, every time he went to visit his friend Tusker. He was glad that the evil Kralahome was finally getting what he deserved. Louis finally felt at home.

In fact he was glad that his mother had brought him to live in the palace. The Prince and Tuptim were now his good friends, as were the other royal children. He practiced kick boxing with the Prince every day. They were both getting so good they had to be careful they didn't hurt each other. Life was never boring, especially with Moonshee around!

When the King was quite recovered he sent for Anna. She found him alone in the empty banquet hall.

"You sent for me, Your Majesty?" she asked.

The King nodded. "Mrs. Anna, you have been a very difficult woman," the King said.

Anna started to answer but he held up his hand. "You have been great help to me, and I wish to make gift."

He took her to the window and made her look out. There outside the palace wall was a perfect English cottage. Rosebushes lined a garden path. Anna stared at it with tears of happiness in her eyes.

"I'm speechless," she stammered.

"For once," the King chuckled.

"At the banquet we didn't dance," the King said to her.

"No, Your Majesty."

"I was looking forward to it," the King said. "Would you accept invitation from King?"

He was surprised when Anna said, "No, Your Majesty." But then she added. "I would gladly accept from a very dear friend."

"You teach me," the King commanded.

Anna showed him how to dance the polka. One two three AND, one two three AND . . . gradually the King learned how to do it. He took Anna in his arms. They started to dance together, twirling around the ballroom, faster and faster. . . .